lulu's
LITTLE
LIBRARY

INTO THE WOODLAND

Written and Illustrated by

lulu's

LITTLE LIBRARY

IN A MYSTICAL FOREST FULL OF WONDERS, THERE WAS A GROUP OF FRIENDS, EACH WITH EXTRAORDINARY TALENTS AND UNIQUE PERSONALITIES.

LET'S WALK AMONG THE TREES AND DISCOVER THE SECRETS THESE WOODLAND CREATURES HOLD.

RUSTLE, RUSTLE!
I'M DARA, THE CURIOUS DEER.

RUSTLE

RUSTLE

WITH MY GRACEFUL STRIDES AND MAJESTIC ANTLERS, I ROAM THE ENCHANTING FOREST, EXPLORING ITS WONDERS AND SEEKING DELICIOUS FOLIAGE TO GRAZE UPON.

DART, DART!
I'M FELIX, THE SLY FOX.

WITH MY FIERY RED FUR AND BUSHY TAIL, I DASH THROUGH THE FOREST WITH SPEED AND AGILITY. I AM AN EXPERT IN CUNNING, USING MY WITS TO OUTSMART OTHERS.

SNEAK, SNEAK!
I'M RILEY, THE SMART RACCOON.

SNEAK
SNEAK

WITH MY AGILE PAWS AND BANDIT-LIKE MASK, I NAVIGATE THE FOREST WITH STEALTH, ALWAYS ON THE LOOKOUT FOR TASTY TREATS AND SHINY TRINKETS TO COLLECT.

HOWL, HOWL!
I'M LUNA, THE WISE WOLF.

AH-OOOOOOOOO

WITH MY KEEN SENSES AND STRONG PACK BOND, I WALK THROUGH THE WILDERNESS,PROTECTING MY FAMILY. I AM A LOYAL AND INTELLIGENT CREATURE, LEADING MY PACK WITH COURAGE.

HOOT, HOOT!
I'M OLIVER, THE VENERABLE OWL.

HOOT
HOOT

WITH MY SILENT FLIGHT AND KEEN EYESIGHT, I PERCH IN THE OLD TREES, OBSERVING THE FOREST CREATURES WITH WISDOM AND PATIENCE. I AM A GUARDIAN OF THE NIGHT.

BUILD, BUILD!
I'M BARRY, THE DILIGENT BEAVER.

BUILD
BUILD

WITH MY STRONG TEETH AND WEBBED FEET, I BUILD INTRICATE DAMS AND SHELTERS ALONG FOREST STREAMS. I AM COOPERATIVE, WORKING WITH MY FAMILY TO CREATE A THRIVING ENVIRONMENT.

GRAZE, GRAZE!
I'M CELESTE, THE GRACEFUL CERVUS.

GRAZE

WITH MY ELEGANT WHITE-SPOTTED COAT AND MAJESTIC ANTLERS, I EMBODY THE BEAUTY OF THE FOREST. I AM A CREATURE OF GRACE AND SERENITY, ADDING TO THE ENCHANTMENT OF THE WOODLAND.

ROAR, ROAR!
I'M BRUNO, THE MIGHTY BEAR.

ROAR

WITH MY POWERFUL STATURE AND THICK FUR, I AM THE RULER OF THE FOREST, YET I AM GENTLE AND CARING WITH MY CUBS. I AM A SYMBOL OF STRENGTH AND HARMONY.

CHATTER, CHATTER!
I'M CHIP, THE TALKATIVE CHIPMUNK.

WITH MY STRIPED COAT AND CHEEK POUCHES, I DART THROUGH THE TREES, ALWAYS COLLECTING AND STORING FOOD FOR THE FUTURE. I AM A BUSY CREATURE.

RABBIT, RABBIT!
I'M FREDDY, THE JUMPY FROG.

RABBIT

WITH MY BULGING EYES AND WEBBED FEET, I HOP THROUGH PONDS AND LILY PADS, ANNOUNCING THE ARRIVAL OF RAIN WITH MY SOOTHING CHORUS. I'M ADAPTING TO LIFE BOTH IN THE WATER AND ON LAND.

ROLL, ROLL!
I'M HAROLD, THE CHEERFUL HEDGEHOG.

WITH SPIKY QUILLS AND A GENTLE ATTITUDE, I CURL UP IN A PROTECTIVE BALL WHEN THREATENED. I AM A CREATURE OF SOFT DEFENSE, WANDERING THROUGH THE WOODS AND SHARING MY POSITIVITY.

SCURRY, SCURRY!
I'M SAL, THE ADVENTUROUS SALAMANDER.

WITH MY THIN BODY AND REGENERATIVE ABILITY, I EXPLORE THE WET FOREST FLOOR AND HIDDEN CREVICES. I THRIVE IN THE MOST ISOLATED CORNERS OF THE FOREST.

CHARGE, CHARGE!
I'M MAX, THE MAGNIFICENT MOOSE.

WITH MY MASSIVE HORNS AND IMPOSING PRESENCE, I ROAM THE FOREST WITH STRENGTH AND CONFIDENCE. I AM A SYMBOL OF AUTHORITY AND NOBILITY.

HOP, HOP!
I'M BELLA, THE LIVELY RABBIT.

WITH MY SOFT FUR AND TWITCHY NOSE, I HOP THROUGH THE UNDERBRUSH, ALWAYS ALERT TO POTENTIAL DANGERS. I AM SPREADING JOY WITH MY ENERGETIC PRESENCE.

CLIMB, CLIMB!
I'M RUBY, THE AGILE RED PANDA.

WITH MY STRIKING COLORS AND AGILE MOVEMENTS, I CLIMB TREES WITH EASE, LOOKING FOR BAMBOO SHOOTS AND FRUIT TO MUNCH ON. I'M AN ELEGANT AND CHARMING CREATURE.

HiSS, HiSS!
I'M SSSYLViA, THE SLEEK SNAKE.

HiSSSSS

WITH MY SLIPPERY FORM AND VIBRATING SCALES, I MOVE SILENTLY
THROUGH THE BUSHES, LIKE A MYSTERIOUS, HIDDEN CREATURE.
I AM A GUARDIAN OF BALANCE.

LEAP, LEAP!
I'M SAM, THE FAST SQUIRREL.

LEAP
LEAP

WITH MY BUSHY TAIL AND ACROBATIC SKILLS, I LEAP FROM BRANCH TO BRANCH, GATHERING NUTS AND SEEDS TO STORE FOR WINTER. I AM A CREATURE OF PREPARATION AND AGILITY.

TAP, TAP!
I'M WOODY, THE DETERMINED WOODPECKER.

TAP
TAP

WITH MY STRONG BEAK, I DRUM ON TREES, SEARCHING FOR INSECTS AND CREATING COZY HOMES IN THE TRUNKS. I AM A TRUE ARCHITECT OF THE FOREST, LEAVING MY MARK WHEREVER I GO.

SNORT, SNORT!
I'M BORIS, THE FORMIDABLE WILD BOAR.

SNORT

WITH MY STURDY TUSKS AND POWERFUL BUILD, I ROAM THE FOREST FLOOR WITH CONFIDENCE. I AM A CREATURE OF STRENGTH AND RESILIENCE, FEARLESSLY PROTECTING MY FAMILY FROM ANY THREAT THAT DARES TO CHALLENGE US.

SPRAY, SPRAY!
I'M STELLA, THE CAUTIOUS SKUNK.

SSSSPRAY

WITH MY DISTINCTIVE BLACK AND WHITE FUR, I MOVE THROUGH THE FOREST WITH CARE, READY TO DEFEND MYSELF IF NECESSARY. I AM A CREATURE OF WARNING, TEACHING OTHERS TO RESPECT BOUNDARIES AND PERSONAL SPACE.

Made in the USA
Middletown, DE
19 November 2024

65038765R00027